Tam in the Garden

by Terry Stingley
illustrated by David Sheldon

Target Skill Short a
High-Frequency Words have, is

Scott Foresman
is an imprint of

I am little Tam.

I have a little hat.

The hat is red.

I have a little mat.

The mat is red.

I have a little garden.

The garden is red.

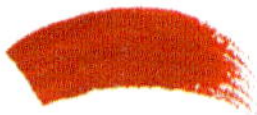